GANDASA : THE LEGEND OF MAULA JUTT

GOLU KUMAR

Copyright © Golu Kumar
All Rights Reserved.

Contents

1

The ring was in place. The onlookers had selected their places to sit. The "Parkoddi" players were encircling the "Dhol that was pounding, their bodies shining with oil. They were dressed in colorful loincloths that were attached firmly to their bodies. To simulate the petals of a lotus flower, thin white straps had been threaded under their oiled hair and toward their heads.

The sound of "Hookas" boiling and people talking could be heard all over the wide field. Analysis of players' previous and present performances as well as discussions of their strengths and weaknesses took place. The renowned wrestling teams weren't yet in the ring. These well-known athletes, who were surrounded by friends and supporters, were receiving oil massages with such vigor and fervour that their bodies sparkled in the setting light as though they had changed into copper sculptures. They then entered the arena, formed a circle around the "Dhol" that was beating, and then ran to their corners to hop and dance as they warmed up for the approaching fight.

"Where is Maula?" was suddenly whispered through the crowd, which quickly turned into a tornado as it traveled around. These people all traveled great distances to witness Maula's prowess; they had come to watch from distant pastures. "Maula's closest pal is also not here." The crowd began to disperse from the ringside and move in the direction of the exits, creating yet another whirlwind. They gathered into a mass that surged and drove others out of the building.

To dissuade the throng from dispersing, the tournament organizers beat the grounds with their sticks, creating clouds of dust in the process. Then, as if a bomb had gone off in the distance, the entire crowd returned to the ringside in silence when someone muttered, "Maula has entered the ring with his best friend."

A Dhol that had been extensively embellished with strings and knots lay in the center of the ring. Maula touched the Dhol after gently circling it three times. When a cry of "Mauley, Mauleya my son, your father has been slain!" struck him on the chest like a "Gandasa" whipping through the air, he had just lifted his palms in the air to shout "Ya Ali."

Maula's uplifted palm whirled like a cobra aiming, and then it appeared as though his feet had developed wings in an instant. His mother's voice chased after him as he ran, "Ranga gutted your father with his Gandasa."

Pandemonium broke out as the ringside crowd broke up, dhols stopped playing, and wrestlers quickly got dressed. The crowd had begun to panic and stampeded in their haste to exit. Maula stamped through the streets, blowing dust through the air as if he were a whirlwind. Far behind him his best friend Taaja followed carrying his and Maula's clothes wrapped in a bundle which he clung to his chest. Even further behind Taaja, a terrified crowd followed anxiously to see what would happen. In the village where nobody dared to walk bare-headed Maula walked wearing only his pink loincloth, piercing through the crowds of people, sheep, and flocks of lambs. When he reached in front of the courtyard of Ranga, he saw a crowd was gathered there. From the crowd that faced him "Peer" Noor Shah emerged and shouted challengingly, "Maula, stop there".

Maula appeared to leap, but his feet suddenly appeared to be firmly planted in place. He then appeared to stand motionless and turn into a statue. "Peer" You won't go any further, Maula, Noor Shah replied to him in his loud, booming voice. Maula remained there panting for some time and stared directly into Peer Noor Shah's eyes. After a lengthy pause, he finally exclaimed, "Why should I live if I don't go any further Peer Jee?"

Peer Jee stated with authority, emphasizing the I in his phrase, "Because I say so."

Despite panting, Maula spoke breathlessly without breaking his stride, "Then rub coal on my face and cut off my nose. I have to avenge my father's death Peer Jee. If it had been the killing of an animal then I would have turned back on your command". Maula shook his neck violently and looked at Ranga's "Chopal ". Ranga and his son "Bhutto" stood chests puffed out, holding their Gandasa's. The Gandasa blades glistened in the glare of the sun.

Ranga's elder son spoke, "Come, on, come. If I don't spill your intestines out with one blow of my Gandasa then my name is not Qaeda. My Gandasa is rash and does not think where it strikes. Pampered sons who play Kabbadi don't avenge their father's death, they weep and go searching for a shroud to wrap his corpse in".

It seemed as if Maula had just been waiting for him to finish speaking. He surged towards the stair of the "Chopal" however, now the crowd from the Kabbadi field had reached there too and stood in his way. Maula's body was slippery from the oil rubbed on his body so he managed to slip out of the hands that tried to grab him, however, the crowd crowded around him like a steel fence which he could not break through.

A section of the throng had also encircled Ranga and his three sons, preventing them from moving forward. The audience suddenly fell silent, leaving the four Gandasas to continue to wave menacingly with swords that shimmered in the waning sunlight like pearls. Peer Noor Shah maneuvered past the mob while holding the Quran in his hands. To the heavens above, he cried, "For the sake of Allah's book, go to your houses; otherwise, whole towns will be demolished, you fools," as he slowly ascended the chopal's stairs. Go, abandon this place for the sake of God and his prophet, for the sake of the Holy Quran.

The crowd began to disperse with their heads bowed. Maula hurriedly took his "laacha" from Taaja and walked off the chopal. Peer Sahib, walked to Maula holding the Quran, and said, "May Allah, give you patience and reward you for the good deed that you did today".

Taija was by Maula's side while he made progress. He turned around and looked back at Ranga's Chopal as he came to the corner of the small street leading to his house. Are you crying, Maula? Taaja sadly questioned. Maula asked, wiping his eyes with his bare arm, "So, should I not even cry now?"

What will the public say? Taaja gave him advice. "Yes, Taajey," Maula said, rubbing his eyes once more with his arm. "That's just what I am anticipating people will say. I'm racing through the streets like a dog with its tail between its legs to go and sob on my mother's shoulder as the flies are feasting on my father's blood.

However, Maula did not cry on his mother's shoulder. He entered his house just as his relatives had decided to take his father's body to the police station. His mother wailing and beating her chest came to him, looked at him, and then said, "You're shameless". She turned her face away from him and went weeping in her husband's body. Maula did not react and looked on with his face fixed in a scowl. He lifted his father's bier and left with his family.

All hell broke loose at Ranga's chopal even though the body had not yet arrived at the police station. When a Gandasa suddenly materialised and slashed Ranga's stomach like a hot knife through butter, he had just down the chopal's stairs and was on the verge of going inside his home. His guts fell in a sizzling heap on the threshold of his home. After a period of chaos and terror, Ranga's sons were able to gather their composure long enough to ride their horses and race into the police station.

When they arrived in the police station yard, they were startled to see the guy they had come to accuse of killing their father already present. Maula was reading prayers from a rosary bead while sitting next to his father's body. By any means necessary, they attempted to submit a FIR with Maula listed as the murderer; however, the constable convinced them to refrain from doing so for fear of losing the identity of their father's genuine killer. He came here a while ago to report the passing of his own father, so now was the moment for them to behave sanely and resist giving in to their fury. How was it possible for him to use a Gandasa to murder your father at your home?"

Eventually cases for both murders were registered, however, due to there being no eye witnesses, the accused were released without charge. The day Maula was released, the first thing after he duly received a loving kiss on his forehead from his mother was to go straight to Taaja's house. He embraced him and said, "If I had not had you and your horse to help me that day, today I would have been swinging from the gallows with a noose around my neck. I swear on your life that after I had cut open Ranga's stomach and mounted your horse I became like the wind. My father's body had not even reached the police station, and I slipped back into the procession without my absence being noticed."

Apart from Taaja and a few close relatives, everyone in the community knew that Maula was Ranga's killer, but no one knew how it had happened. Everything went back to normal, but one day a rumour started to circulate in the hamlet that Qadir, Ranga's son, had actually slain Maula's father. Ranga had merely boasted. This was the only subject that was discussed at the gathering places, sitting areas, cafes, and everywhere else where people congregated. Everyone learned in the morning that Qadir had been discovered on his rooftop in such a state of decay that when his brothers Phulla and Ghulla attempted to lift his body, his head had fallen off and continued to roll until it hit the gutter.

Maula was detained once more after a report was made. The cops made every effort to get him to admit to the crime. He stood on a sheet of steel in the scorching sun, breathing in the stench of burning chiles. God alone knows how many nights he was awakened by being jabbed with a stick as soon as he fell asleep. Maula persevered despite all of these hardships. He declined to admit to the crime. After many months, he was reluctantly released despite the Maliks' best attempts to pressure the police continually.

As a free man, Maula went back to his village. His mother rushed over to greet him as he entered the courtyard of his home, kissing him on the forehead and saying, "Two still remain my son. I won't refer to you as my son until you leave no one behind who will use Ranga's name. Repay the debt I owe you for the milk I fed you and that gave you energy. Your veins also carry your father's blood. Establish your worthiness to carry his name. As you can see, I prevented your Gandasa from rusting; it still sparkles.

Maula now became the terror of his neighbourhood. His moustache grew until it curled at each end, in his ears hung large golden earrings, his long hair smelt with fragranced oil. A crescent shaped comb made from ivory shone on his forehead. When he walked through the streets, at least half a metre of his cummerbund trailed behind him marking wherever he went. A thin cotton scarf hung on his shoulder. Often one end of it would fall on the floor and scrape on the floor and would keep scraping till it wore thin. In Maula's hand, there was always a long stick that stood taller than him; whenever he sat on the street corner or crossroad, he rested this stick on his knee. No passer by dared to ask Maula to move the stick aside.

People would come, stare at the stick and at Maula, then turn around and go another way if the stick ever managed to get jammed between two opposing walls. Maula's customary haunts, the streets, were no longer even visited by men or kids. Because nobody dared to jump over Maula's stick, the situation grew worse.

Maula was sitting in the street when a young stranger passed by. Maula was aimlessly poking his stick into the wall across from him. When he arrived, the stranger leapt over Maula's stick. Immediately furious, Maula removed the Gandasa blade from his pocket and attached it to the stick. "Stop son, do you realise whose stick you have leapt over," he yelled at the stranger. The owner is Maula. The Gandasa-Welder Maula.

After hearing Maula's name, the stranger grew pale and nervously said, "I did not know, Maula." Maula put the blade in his pocket after removing it. Then he said, "Be on your way then," as he softly poked the strangers' stomachs with one end of his stick. He then sat down after laying his stick out again from one end of the street to the other.

The fashion of Maula's village and the surrounding area spread from there as a result of his attire, walk, moustache, and most all, his carefree attitude. Maula did, however, have a lengthy staff, which did not become fashionable. Nobody feared to cross it since it was so long and glistened with oil, was ornamented with lotus flowers, and was sealed at either end by steel caps that made music when they struck the road's pebbles. The Gandasa blade, which was in his pocket, was frequently ornamented on it. The blade that his mother could not let to rust for fear that it might lessen Maula's will for vengeance.

The people claimed that Maula was sitting in the streets looking for Ghulla and Phulla with his stick extended and his Gandasa blade concealed. Phulla joined the army and relocated after Qada's passing and Maula's release, while Ghulla sought safety from the region's well-known rope-pulling champion Chauhdary Muzaffar Ilahee. Ghulla would search the banks of the rivers Chenab and Ravi for cows and buffaloes to steal, just like Chauhdary's other workers. Chauhdary Muzaffar would sell them and use the money to throw extravagant parties for the powerful, including ministers and politicians, with whom he had his picture shot for use in publications like newspapers and magazines.

Following their track would be Ravi and Chenab's trail finders who had looked into the missing animals. The trail finders would say to themselves, "I had already suspected this," as these tracks got closer to Chauhdary Muzaffar's village. They were aware that if they followed the trails to the Chauhdary's home, eventually people would start trying to follow the trail finders' last known whereabouts but would be unsuccessful. They would trek through to the coast out of fear for the Chauhdary and then come back claiming, "Their trail turns cold here."

Chauhdary Muzaffar and his outstretched arms had been mentioned by Maula. While he was waiting for Ranga's two sons to emerge, he believed that only Chauhdary Muzaffar had the bravery to leap over his stick in the entire region.

Like a big brother, Taaja reprimanded Maula, advising him to at least take care of his fields. What was the point of sitting with a stick in the streets from sunrise to sunset while having slaves and lackeys surrounding him waiting for his orders? Maybe you aren't aware of it, but you ought to be aware that mothers have been using you to frighten their kids for your own good. In order to curse another girl, girls spit when they hear her name.

Maula received a stern talking-to from Taaja, who advised him to at least take care of his fields. What good was it to sit in the streets with a stick from sunrise to sunset while having slaves and lackeys surrounding him waiting for his orders? Perhaps you are unaware of this, but you need to be aware of it for your own protection because mothers have been using you to frighten their kids. If a girl wants to curse someone, she says, "May Allah marry you to Maula." Girls spit when they hear your name. Do you hear me?

Oh Taaja, just go away. He had undergone a transformation as a result of Maula's forging in fire. Have you gathered all the slurs from the hamlet to hurl at my feet, he demanded? Making a friendship work is a difficult undertaking that not everyone can manage. Why have you come to lead me astray if you can no longer handle the responsibilities of friendship? My Gandasa's thirst has not yet been sated. Go." He called a servant from the house across the street after striking the floor with his Gandasa. You still haven't filled up the hookah, moron. Had you dozed off? the hookah bowl, please.

Taaja turned away. At the corner of the street he turned and looked at Maula as if he would burst crying at his young death. Maula was looking at him from the corner of his eyes. He got up and walked over to Taaja dragging his stick behind him. He stood next to him and said, "Taaja it seems as if you are pitying me because once upon a time I was your friend. Our friendship is over now though. If you cannot support me then of what use is your friendship to me? My father's blood is not so cheap that it can be avenged by the death of just Ranga and his son. My Gandasa has yet to smite his granddaughters and grandsons. Our ways have parted. Don't pity me, if someone pities me it dulls my Gandasa's blade. Go."

Maula came back and took a seat. The embers blew and dispersed when he pulled the hookah bowl away from his servant. On his hand, a blazing ember landed and briefly lit up the area. The servant attempted to dust it off Maula's hand, but Maula violently smacked his hand away, causing the man to fall to the ground in agony. He stepped away to the side while squeezing his palm firmly between his thighs. He pities me, the bastard, yelled Maula. The hookah bowl was snatched up and thrown at the wall by him. Then, storming out with his stick in hand.

People were astonished and whispered to one another when they observed Maula sitting at a new street corner.

They decided it would be best to walk away from him and disperse after that. Women returning from the well with pitchers were unable to pass his stick since it was spread over the tiny street, and they could only exclaim in despair. Everyone believed that Maula was seeking blood. Maula was observing an eagle perched on the mosque's minaret while those around him questioned what he was doing.

The sound of his stick striking the pebbles startled him from his thoughts. A young girl had taken up his stick and was leaning it against the wall, which startled him. She was currently occupied with gathering the long, red chiles that had fallen from the bunch on her head as she had bowed over. Her brazenness left Maula speechless. She a woman had set his stick aside like it was a dirty rag and was now sitting contentedly in front of him selecting her chiles, so forget about jumping over the stick.

Do you know whose stick you have touched? Maula yelled indignantly. Are you aware of who I am? She put up her hands and said, "You," as she stuffed the peppers into her bundle.

Outraged Do you know whose stick you touched, Maula yelled? Do you recognise me? You look to be some grouch, she added as she put the chillies in her bundle and lifted her hands.

Enraged Maula erupted. She stood up as well and stated softly, "That's why I didn't smash your stick on your head, I felt empathy for you. You looked so lost and lonely." You have sympathy for me? Maula cried out. The girl said, "Maula?" while holding her parcels in both hands and expressing some astonishment.

Maula proudly said, "Yes, Maula the Gandasa-wielder." She gave a shaky smile before entering the roadway. After remaining motionless for a while, Maula heaved a long sigh and sat down against the wall. He spotted an elderly woman approaching from the opposite side after spreading his stick against the opposing wall. She halted when she spotted Maula. Come Aunty, come I won't bite you, Maula called as he raised his stick and set it aside. The woman arrived and exclaimed, "What falsehoods people tell, people say that wherever Maula sits even a mad dog dare not go there," as she went by him. However, you took up your stick for me.

Who made that claim? Maula stepped up and questioned inquisitively. Everyone in the village agrees on this. They could only talk about this when I was at the well earlier. However, I can personally attest that Maula Bukhsh exists.

Maula was now too far away to hear, though. The young girl had just left the roadway when he leaped into it. He moved quickly till he noticed her gently walking at the end of a street. Women who were sitting in their courtyards came to their doorsteps as he started to run, and kids went up onto the roofs of the houses. The street sprinting Maula did was perceived as the beginning of a catastrophe. The girl turned around and stood where she was after hearing Maula's footsteps. A few chillies fell from her bundle onto her feet like smouldering embers as she did nothing more than hold it with both hands.

"I won't harm you in any way," "I will not harm you. Don't be afraid," shouted Maula.

I didn't stop out of fear, may my adversaries be scared, the girl retorted.

Just tell me that, who are you, he urged as he approached Maula after she had stopped. A little smile appeared on her face. Maula Bukhsh, he heard an elderly woman say behind him. Rajo, the youngest son of Ranga, is engaged to her.

Maula looked in disbelief at Rajo. He noticed Rajo standing close to Ranga and his entire family. His hand reached for his Gandasa in the pocket but immediately collapsed. Rajo made a U-turn and retreated slowly.

Rajo, hold on, here, take your peppers, Maula flung his stick to the side. Rajo halted, and Maula knelt down to pick up each and every chilli he could find. He questioned Rajo, "You felt empathy for me, didn't you Rajo?" as he tucked them into his bundle. "

Rajo stepped away as her expression grew grim. Maula turned and proceeded in his direction. When the elderly woman called, "Maula Bakhsh, you have left your stick behind, here it is," he had only gone a short way. When Maula came back, he asked the elderly woman, "Aunty, this girl Rajo does she reside around here? She is a new face to me here.

The elderly woman responded, "She is from here and not from here too." After losing his two young kids, her father erected a modest cabin 2-3 furlongs away in the fields since he could no longer bring the plough from his house to the fields every day. There, Rajo resides with her father. She merely visits the village once every three to four days to make purchases.

Maula could only respond, "Hmm," and she left. The rumour that Maula had left his stick somewhere and forgotten about it quickly spread throughout the community. Rajo's name was occasionally brought up in these chats but was quickly ignored. Rajo was after all the fiancé of Ranga's son, and the sole connection between Maula and Ranga's household was through the Gandasa. Nobody wanted either side to claim that they were being slandered because, above all else, who doesn't value their life?

After this incident, Maula vanished from the public view. He spent the entire day digging the soil out of the flowerbed while sitting at home. If he ever left the house, he would spend some time in the fields and grazing pastures before going back. His mother was taken aback by his actions, but she said nothing to him. She was aware of Maula's fury and the weight of his crimes, which weighed heavily on his mind. of those he had committed and those he hadn't been able to.

Ramadan, a month of fasting, was currently in effect. The drums that had signalled its coming had stopped beating and gone silent. For Sehri, homes throughout the town were getting ready. yoghurt churning makes a noise

Ramadan, a month of fasting, was in session. The drums that had been beating to announce its arrival had stopped. The village's residences were getting ready for Sehri . Like the enigmatic bells that rung in temples, the sound of churning yoghurt and the girdling of Rotis permeated the air.

Maula's mother too had turned on the stove was cooking Roti. Maula lay on a Charpai on the roof staring at the sky. Suddenly, in a nearby street, a commotion broke out. Maula armed his stick with the Gandasa and leapt from the roof into the street. He ran towards where the noise was coming from. Along the way from every house people emerged with lanterns and the noise only grew louder. When Maula reached where the commotion was he saw three strangers armed with spears and swords shepherding a herd of cows and buffaloes through the village streets. The village guard had tried to stop them but they had swore at him and said, "This herd belongs to Chauhdary Muzaffar Illahi. This is only a lowly village, when his herds pass through the streets of Lahore even there nobody dares to whimper"

Maula had the impression that Chahudary Muzaffar himself had entered the village street and was attempting to seize his Gandasa. Maula declared angrily, "This Chauhdary herd will not travel through my hamlet, regardless of whether the herd is owned by Chauhdary Muzaffar or a certain minister. Leaving the animals here and going quietly is the wisest course of action, if you know what it is. He dropped his stick, letting the light from the lights catch the Gandasa blade. Maula said, "Go."

"Go tell your Chahudary Muzaffar that Maula the Gandasa wielding sends his greetings," Maula said as he started to herd the animals while holding his stick to one side. Now leave the area. The outsiders noticed that the crowd's countenance had altered due to Maula and were now enraged. They decided it would be best to go in silence. The herd was brought to his home by Maula, and as Sehri was eating, he informed his mother, "These stupid animals are our guests; their owners will arrive from elsewhere in a few days. The honour of the community is also my honour, mum.

The very following day, the owners showed up. They were underprivileged farmers and farmworkers who had walked for endless miles begging for help from trail blazers before reaching Maula's community. The owners had been considering what they would do if their animals wound up in Chauhdary Muzaffar's territory the entire time. The entire town had gathered in Maula's street when he gave them their animals back. Rajo was one of them; she had a clay pot set on top of a cloth that she had fastened around her head. Rajo also started to depart as the gathering dispersed. He questioned her, "You have come to the village after many days," as she passed by Maula. This is a question, right?

"Why?" She spoke in a way that suggested she was trying to convince him that she had no fear. "I arrived yesterday, as well as the days before that. To purchase some garlic, I came early in the week. I visited the Hakeem with Baba the day before yesterday. I arrived yesterday without a purpose, and today I'm here to sell ghee.

"Why did you arrive yesterday without a purpose?" Maula eagerly enquired.

Well, I had the urge to come, so I went to meet my buddies and left. Why?"

Dejectedly, Maula responded, "No reason. Then an idea struck him. Do you plan to sell this ghee?

"Yes, I must sell it, but not to you," she said.

"Why?"

"The blood of my relatives is all over your hands."

Maula recalled that he had forgotten his stick in the hallway and his Gandasa under his pillow. His hands started to itch, so he grabbed a rock from the ground and started rubbing it between his fingers. Maula frantically said, "Look Rajo, my hands are covered in blood and heaven knows how much more blood they are yet to be coated in, but you have to sell your ghee and I need to buy ghee," as Rajo turned to leave. If you don't want to sell it to me, you can sell it to my mother instead. Okay, let's go, Rajo stated after giving it some thought.

Walking in front of her was Maula. He had the impression that Rajo was examining his back and muscles as he walked. When he turned around and noticed that she was watching chicks picking at birdfeed on the sidewalk, he yelled, "These chicks are mine."

They might be, Rajo said. Now that Maula was in the courtyard, she commanded, "Mother, get all this ghee. I have visitors coming in a few days."

Rajo took the pot off her head and removed the cloth covering it a bit so that the old woman could smell the ghee. Maula's mother however had gone inside to bring the scales. Maula saw that Rajo had golden locks on her temples; her eyelashes were bent like longbows and could touch her eyebrows if she raised them. Her eyelashes had specks of dirt on them and there were small drops, the size of pinheads, of sweat on her nose. Her nostrils were in such a state that it did not seem as if she smelt ghee but instead the fragrance of roses. On the bridge of her lips there was sweat too and between her lower lip and chin there was a mole, stuck as if it would blow away if you blew on it.

Her ear was adorned with silver chandelier earrings that swung like clusters of grapes on a vine. An earring was entangled in a lock. The Gandasa-wielding Maula had the want to carefully untangle it before either tucking it behind her ear or letting it dangle there. He also had the urge to spread it out on his hand and count each individual hair. When his mother pulled out the scales and sat down next to Rajo, Maula was deep in concentration.

"Aunty, check the ghee first by smelling or touching it. This morning, it was freshly made. You should still be able to smell it, Rajo remarked, even though it is still warm from boiling.

I won't smell it, daughter, I promise. His mother declared that her fast would be invalidated. She then gave Rajo a close glance before locking her gaze on him. She questioned, "You are Ghulam Ali's daughter aren't you?" after a time.

"Yes."

"Get away from here!" The mother of Maula scooped up the scales, got to her feet, and threw them away. "How indiscreet of you to enter my home! You have the gall to trade ghee with us when the only form of exchange that is permitted between us is blood. Leave." "My darling you, don't buy Ghee from those that you should smite with your Gandasa," she murmured, turning to face Maula. It's Ghulla's fiancee here. Ghulla, son of Ranga

With her face hot with rage, Rajo hastily covered her pot, took it up, and questioned, "Do you have hearts in your breasts or poppy seeds?"

Maula got the impression that Rajo and his mother had each smacked him across the face separately. After Rajo left, he went and laid down on the charpai on the roof under the shady sun since he felt degraded. He spent several hours there. He was crying when his mother arrived to call him down. "Maula, do you sound upset? Maula responded, "Should I not even cry then? " his mother asked in amazement. "

His mother's head began to spin as she sat down unsteadily. She looked to her son's query for a response to her own query. Maula no longer even visited him at his house. He spent the entire day relaxing at Noora's tea shop at the

His mother's head began to spin as she sat down unsteadily. She looked to her son's query for a response to her own query. Maula no longer even visited him at his house. He would stay at Noora's tea shop at the bus station all day. The youth and children of the entire hamlet would congregate there every day before dusk when the coach from the city would come. Everyone would visit Noora's for tea while asking the drivers about the most recent events in the city.

On his charpai, Maula would recline distantly and watch the sky while sitting alone. They would even bring the hookah from close by because everyone had grown accustomed to Maula by this point. No one, however, would dare to touch.

On his charpai, Maula would recline distantly while observing the sky. By this time, everyone was accustomed to Maula; they would even bring the hookah from nearby. Nobody, however, dared to jump over or touch his stick, which was stretched taut from his charpai to the coach nearby.

One day, a silence descended upon the station as the evening coach pulled up and its passengers exited. Everyone had gradually become silent, like if death had arrived. Ghulla, the son of Ranga, alighted from the coach, and four tall, broad, hulking men followed. The five separated and began to converse alone.

When Maula became aware of the quiet surrounding him, he sat up on his Charpai. Near Noora's store, the crowd had collapsed, and Ghulla was standing directly across from him, pointing. As soon as he pulled his Gandasa out of his pocket, he rapidly swung his legs off the charpai. He attached it to his stick and yelled, "Noora, get the hookah here." Noora went into his store after purchasing the hookah and placing it nearby with shaking hands.

The five newcomers regarded Maula while standing apart from the coach. Maula drew deeply from the hookah and carelessly puffed smoke into the air.

Gulla cried out to him, "Mauley."

After another drag, "Speak," Maula directed its smoke at Ghulla.

We're here to share a message with you.

"Say it now, go ahead."

"Set away your Gandasa, we are unarmed,"

Maula motioned with his stick, "Here." The five approached him in slow motion. The crowd resembled something that had clung to the wall. To have a better view of the gathering, the kids had moved further back and ascended the potter's stoop.

"What's that?" Maula enquired of Ghulla. Did you stop Chauhdary's herd when Ghulla, who had now arrived close to Maula, asked?

Maula nodded indifferently. "Yes," she continued.

In the corner of his eyes, Ghulla glanced at his friend before clearing his throat. For this, Chauhdary Muzaffar has sent you a prize. He instructed us to present you with your award in front of the entire community.

"Reward?" Maula was taken aback. "What's going on here?"

Gulla hit Maula's face with a crack that reverberated through the audience and said, "This is what it's about," before speeding away.

In one continuous motion, Maula grabbed up his stick and leapt for the charpai after reacting as though he had been shocked. In the light of the setting sun, the Gandasa glistened like a flame. The five newcomers moved away at a speed that was not humanly possible, but Ghulla fell due to loose stones close to the coaches. Maula quickly closed in on him. The jumping Maula came to a stop, and the man elevated his Gandasa before bringing it down and stopping it at an angle close to Ghulla. Slowly, the enthralled audience moved forward; the kids had also left the stoop for a better vantage point. Noora left his store with her mouth open.

Ghulla appeared to be trying to hide as far away from Maula as he could by digging his fingers and feet into the ground. Maula, who had appeared to be in shock, moved forward as everyone watched and threw his Gandasa in the direction of his charpai. "Give Chauhdary my regards and tell him I have got his award, I will come to give him the receipt for it myself," he added, carefully picking up Ghulla off the ground.

He slowly dusted Ghullas's clothing, fixed the turban's crooked crest, and continued, "I would have given you the receipt but you haven't become a bridegroom yet. Therefore, proceed and complete your tasks.

Ghulla gently turned and walked away with his head bent. Maula approached his charpai while moving carefully. The crowd retreated as he moved forward. His mother, who was running toward the potter's house and shouting like a banshee and hitting her head, appeared as he attempted to sit down. "Ghulla slapped you and you did nothing to him," she yelled in an unrestrained passion as she drew closer to Maula. You were once my courageous son. Why did your Gandasa fail to kill him? You...." She abruptly stopped striking her head and asked, "Maula, but are you crying?" in a gentle voice as if she were speaking from a far continent.

The Gandasa-wielding Maula sat down on the charpai and used his arm to rub his eyes. Then, sounding like a young child, she said, "So, should I not even cry now?"

The term "Gandasa" describes both a blade and the weapon created by fusing a blade and a stick.